To Rich – JL
To Zohra with love – DA

First published in Great Britain 2016 by Egmont UK Limited
The Yellow Building, 1 Nicholas Road, London W11 4AN
www.egmont.co.uk
Text copyright © Jill Lewis 2016
Illustrations copyright © Deborah Allwright 2016
The moral rights of the author and illustrator have been asserted.
ISBN 978 1 4052 7821 8
A CIP catalogue record for this title is available from the British Library.

EGMONT
we bring stories to life

Hooray
for
Knickers

Jill Lewis
&
Deborah Allwright

EGMONT

King Grouchy
was always grumpy,
so he didn't have many friends.

Even when he was supposed to
be having fun he was still grumpy!

Prince Jolly, however, had lots of friends and the king wanted to be one of them, so he invited him for a swim at the Palace.

JOLLY ROYAL NEWS FLASH···

King Grouchy wanted everything to be perfect for the visit.

The day came and King Grouchy got out of bed
on the wrong side. This put him in a seriously bad mood.

All the servants hid to keep out of his way.

So King Grouchy shouted the order:

"Prince Jolly is coming for a swim!
And he's going to be my new best friend!

We need floats, deck chairs and silky slippers!
Get everything
and get it now!"

The Royal Butler listened hard
from the cupboard under the stairs.

"What?!"

He panicked and yelled the order:

"Prince Jolly is coming
for a swim!
He's going to be the king's new
best friend. They need boats,
black bears and silly flippers.

Help me get everything now!"

The Royal Footman strained
to hear from the hayloft.

"What?!"

He panicked and yelled:

"The king's got a new best friend
who's coming for a swim!
They need goats, a sack of pears
and smelly kippers.
Help me get everything now!"

The Royal Gardener struggled to hear from the greenhouse.

"What?!"

He panicked and yelled:

"The king's best friend in the world is coming for a swim. They need coats, stacks of hares and sparkly stickers.
Help me get everything now!"

The Royal Maid could hardly hear from behind the washing basket and was puzzled.

"What?!" she asked.

"He needs skipping ropes?
A funfair?

And everyone needs
frilly knickers?

Oh well, if that's what the king's best
friend in the whole wide world wants . . ."

At last, Prince Jolly arrived.

"We're going to have a lovely time,"
King Grouchy said proudly. "I've ordered everything we need."
And he led the prince out onto the balcony to show him.

They gaped at the flippers, the kippers,
the stickers and all the frilly knickers!

. . . the boats, the goats, the coats and the ropes.
They gawped at the funfair, the bears,
the pears and the hares.

"What?!"

Prince Jolly exclaimed.

Prince Jolly burst out laughing!
"I had no idea you have so much fun here," he beamed.
"Best friends need matching frilly knickers
and we need them now!"

King Grouchy turned redder
and redder and **redder**.

He was about to **explode** when . . .

They looked at...

King Grouchy couldn't believe he had a best friend. "You're right," he chuckled, "we do have fun here.

Hooray for knickers!

"...Let the party begin!"